Published by arrangement with HarperCollins
Publishers Ltd in 1998
All Rights Reserved

Printed in Spain

Published by
Mantra Publishing
5 Alexandra Grove
London N12 8NU
http://www.mantrapublishing.com

جاء من الفضاء

It Came From Outer Space

Written by TONY BRADMAN Illustrated by CAROL WRIGHT

Arabic Translation by Azza Habashi

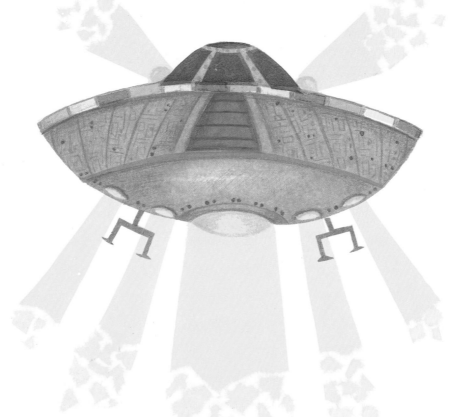

mantra

كنا جميعاً فى المدرسة، نعمل بجد، عندما...

We were all in school, working
hard, when...

إرتطمت سفينة فضاء غريبة بالسقف.

لقد كانت مفاجأة عظيمة!

أصابنا الرعب عندما...

...an alien space ship crashed
through the roof.
It was quite a surprise!
We were frightened when...

بدأ باب سفينة الفضاء يفتح،

وصرخنا فزعاً عندما صعد الوحش.

لقد كان مرعباً.

...the space ship's door started to
open, and we all screamed when
The Monster climbed out.
It was terrifying.

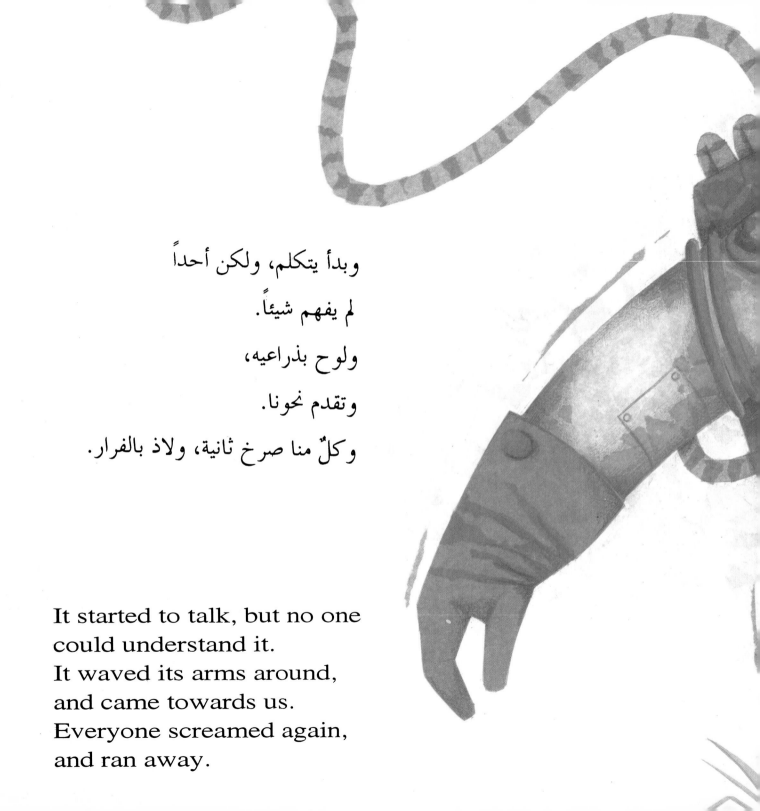

وبدأ يتكلم، ولكن أحداً
لم يفهم شيئاً.
ولوح بذراعيه،
وتقدم نحونا.
وكلٌ منا صرخ ثانية، ولاذ بالفرار.

It started to talk, but no one
could understand it.
It waved its arms around,
and came towards us.
Everyone screamed again,
and ran away.

هرول خلفنا نحو الملعب.

حتى حوصرنا في ركن.

It lumbered after us into the playground.
We were trapped in a corner.

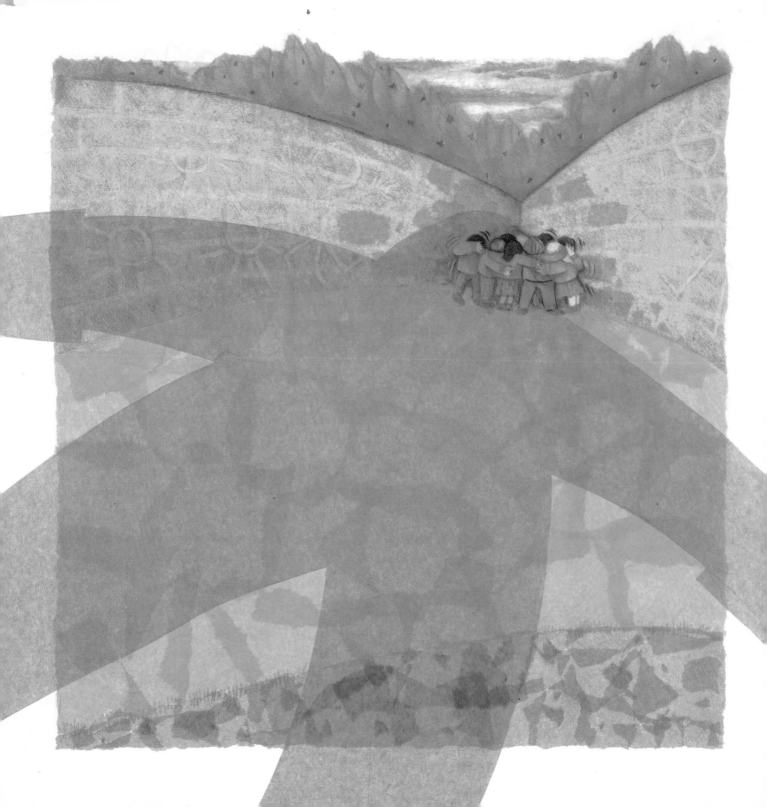

ظل المخلوق المرعب يتكلم ويلوح بذراعيه.
ثم خلع خوذته.

The Monster kept talking and
waving its arms around.

And then it took its helmet off.

لقد كان منظراً مرعباً.

وجه هذا المخلوق المرعب كان مقززاً

وإضطررنا للنظر إلى الناحية الأخرى.

وأصيبت مدرستنا بالإغماء.

It was a horrible sight.
The Monster's face was so
disgusting we had to look the
other way.
Our teacher fainted.

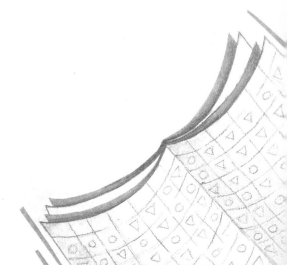

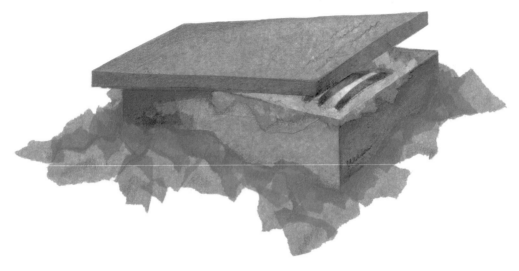

ومع ذلك ظهر أن هذاالمخلوق المرعب لطيفاً جداً.
حيث أهدانا هدية. ثم أدخلنا فى سفينته الفضائية.
حتى أنه فرجنا على بعض الصور لمنزله.

The Monster turned out to be quite nice
though. It gave us a present. It showed us
inside its space ship. It even showed us
some pictures of its home.

لقد شعرت مدرستنا بتحسن الآن، فأخذت صورة للمخلوق المرعب بآلة التصوير.

ثم كان عليه أن يرحل.

Our teacher who was feeling better now, took a picture of The Monster with her camera.

Then it had to go.

كنَّا حزانا لنرى هذا المخلوق يطير
بعيداً. ولوحنا بأيدينا جميعاً.
لقد كان مخلوقاً ودوداً،
مع أن شكله كان قبيحاً جداً.
وددنا لو أنه يعود إلينا مرة أخرى.

We were sad to see The
Monster fly away. We all waved.
It was a very friendly monster,
even though it was so ugly. We
hope it comes back soon.

على الأقل لقد حصلنا على صورة لهذا المخلوق لنتذكره بها...

At least we've got a picture of
The Monster to remember it by...